W9-ACM-457

Joan & The Man

TODD RYKACZEWSKI

WORD REVOLT, LLC. ATLANTIC BEACH, FL

Joan and The Man

Chapter One: Joan, Part One

Joan walks into a dressing room at a local
boutique with nine bras and a yellow dress. She closes
the door while the attendant hangs a number seven on
the outside of the room. Her toes danced on the polished
floor while size six and a half feet lift and twist in
garment removal. Only about a foot and a half or her
legs show, a foot to just below the knee to be exact.
Joan's feet lift and hobble as one of the black bras fall off,
landing lace on top of her feet. In a flash she picks the
garment up. Joan's leg tenses and then relaxes over the
next twenty minutes.

The attendant watches me watch Joan and
abruptly asks in a way to break my focus, "Sir, do you
need help?" Slow to answer, The Man replies, "No, help
is not needed to watch my wife." Embarrassed in a way
that was rude enough for the both of them, the attendant
wrinkles her face and removes herself from the scene.
Small feet dancing on the floor reappear, almost in
rewind as everything that had to come off to try the bras
on now was going back on.

Later Joan would explain to The Man that this
particular fashion is called a *bralette*. Imposed propaganda
to younger hip girls such as Joan or those tired of wires
and being hot. Joan walked away with two out of the

nine chest constraints and no dress. The remaining promenade showed this clothing's popularity while highlighting other functional fashions. Holding hands, the two made their way to dinner, a quick comedy, and then there was not much more time on a Sunday for drinks before bed.

Off, Joan felt at peace to sleep on the couch just feet from the desk in the gallery. This particular desk is from the fifties and known as a tank desk. Made of thick steel, it held rust while performing ageless function. Joan always slept behind, in front or on the sofa behind the tank desk. To settle four feet away for one night was hard but she understood there was a story to write.

Neither of the two owned clothing that was completely free of paint. The Man would always be slightly dirty from work and Joan was okay with that. The gallery would also have some fringe and that would help mask the overall condition. Nightly parties of souls would break and cause a mess. At first she thought that this was intentional in a way to hurt. Over time there was a definition for the mediation of the space that was easier to live with.

The gallery was not a home or heaven and definitely not a studio. Word Revolt Art Gallery was an adult playground. When playing, messes are made if the playing is free. To be truly free, the moment has to be liquid and in being liquid, anything goes. Like the night of the broken china, on the newly painted black floor, that created a celestial universe.

The night of the broken plate, the two sat and ate dinner that was prepared as usual, by Joan. The food sat posed on porcelain plates. The dishes had little blue and red flowers hand painted around the edges. This was the first time in years the hardware had been used. Prior to that they sat stuck in a wooden cabinet in a neighbor's garage that had been long torn down.

Joan and The Man finished their food and digest the sunset and the parcels for some time. Joan smiled. The Man smiled and in a long moment had many conversations. Once the fuel broke while the weight lifted there was an ample distinction for peaceful but needed pause from air consumption. The Man cleared what was left of the food off the dish the best a metal fork would allow with poise and a sip of craft beer.

The Man extended a hand attached to the end of an arm, an extremity holding a gently used plate. Looking at Joan with a sense of destruction, he said, "Celestial universe, with a few flowers." Then tossed the fragile disk over the black cement floor. The two occupants, gallery and china plate, would never piece together that night. All they had when the sun came up was a galaxy of shattered white specs that translated into a mess for Joan to clean and one less dish to wash.

Morning would rise, with a high tide of rainfall on the desert floor of the gallery. This day would join all days in collaboration while Joan jumped up to make coffee. The Man, soaked in blankets, fought the lamp and it's one light bulb bought from the dollar store. The Man hated all days that had him work but Saturdays plagued him. As PTSD would on any individual with a mind or head that would fit a well-prepared hat.

On each day after Friday, Joan, The Man and Duke the newly adopted dog, would file into an electric car that was now vintage and make the seven AM pilgrimage to RAM, Riverbend Arts Market, or as he thought, Rodents At Mercy. As the reader might not be from Jacksonville, Florida, this particular scam was held under a highway onramp that acted as a noose on a perfectly polluted river. Painters alongside crafters and creatives alike would all conjure under this bridge to pay fifty-four American dollars, in hopes to sell their toils.

Impulsive hobbyists found daydreaming about recognition that might replace their drinking day job and sexual desires of the continuously let down middle class. Classy art faire vendors pretended to be gypsies while paying for police protection under a waterfall of pollution that was originally intended for the homeless.

Tiny greenhouses stuffed with moss in round fishbowls sell for twenty bucks and in turn tin silver rings turn higher cash slower. Caricatures go for five dollars but after tip will exceed fifteen. Painters, photographers, tarot readers, with a mix of small batch farmers that go for the planet and passion as they are lucky to break even and get high shortly after.

Nine-thirty to three food trucks make a profit along with the cops and the painful anxious bosses who have to look The Man in the eye. A difficult feat made more so after The Man adopted the third family member, Duke, a seventy-pound Black Foot yellow Labrador Retriever that had been predestined to join the artists of Word Revolt Art Gallery. All of this in reflection to the caveman predicting the necessary popularity of vandalism alongside art in the home, Duke was in fact a foreshadowed pet.

Three weeks before Duke's arrival, Joan and The Man drove to the place called RAM for the first time. In blue chalk on one of the bridge's giant cement pillars there was graffiti reading, "The Man loves dogs." The Man being the 2,422nd most popular name in the US in 2017, down 1,072 from 2016 but still holding the hashtag, 2422. Regardless, Duke is a fine walking companion, though any companion would do while Joan regurgitated caricatures to the easily amused mass.

Healthy never started in a 1970's vintage school chair. To clarify, let's go over to the Word Revolt booth. Towards Joan, there was a blue vinyl tent topper, lovingly painted after some direction from The Man. Under the vinyl were Joan, an artist stool, table and easels with one advertisement for the gallery and others for custom grown art. The type of art that came from rooted torture of some vice once holding a heart to a stranger that only knew how to enflame candles.

Small stuff included drawing paper, felt pens and business cards with the addition of a book that was recognizable by the older crowd and only held entertainment at the start. Amongst this was a green elder chair, had three original feet with the fourth grounded to the floor. This chair held the Earth, even as a subway refracts to meet the rotting wood under the tracks of any train. One could rock from right to back to left or simply sit and ride the half-inch gap.

Matters of Duke

The only living detail that changed over time in the artist's life was the third living brut and a slight creature of comfort that proved violent to strangers. Duke was a loving four-legged killing machine that only loved The Man. For everyone else, Duke was a mouth with teeth that proved the depth of his judging eyes. A canine of sorts in search for an open bed but vacant world where he could hunt small game and never be bothered by a population.

Regardless of the people's skin tone, sex or nature of their walking draft, anger or fear wasn't the issue as much as maltreatment or hunger left lingering from a previous owner. Yes, attacking was the skip in his bite and the game in a tail wag. The very hung tongue that

6

excited a day out amongst victims, he was less a companion and more of a hunter of the inborn human fear of animals with teeth. Fortunately as a leash was provided to Joan and The Man there was never a prime opportunity for teeth to marry flesh. Actually, Duke's time with the artists was an exciting time of yelling, "No Duke!" and, "Good boy!"

On a particularly foggy day that hung over the eyes in a white mesh fashion, Duke would find the next chapter of the safari worth leaving the gallery. The two artists sat perched under the blue tent with Joan under the front portion while Duke with The Man under the rear side of the temporary roof. Joan had just swallowed an allergy pill that she described as, "Just enough to clear the palette of what is going on."

This time they were all at an art gathering called Beaches Art Walk. The man had a coffee mixed unfairly with Irish whiskey. This particular event went on from five PM to nine PM and was set a simple bock back from the Atlantic Ocean, where *walkers*, those who walk at art walks, could hear the crash of the ocean while eating shrimp and causing artists to socialize.

The reader should know that those stuck on the business side of a booth are often prisoners to the walkers and the conversations they wish to pursue. The booth attendee was on the fixed smile side while the walkers had the forward motion of cash.

Still the day came to around seven PM, the time The Man would walk over to the blue hybrid car and take a mid Thursday nap with Duke. The wind was cool with a typical hot sun as to provide perfect opportunity for the descent of the car's windows. The time had gone by but how much was uncertain due to the deep truth of The Man's slumber. Tucked under the couple's picnic blanket with his worn fedora over closed eyes, there wasn't much that could be noticed even if noticing much was desired.

The Man had worked all week from rise to fall with the perfect amount of liquor, still at half-life, roaming the halls of his bodily system. Duke on the other hand was young and fully rested, with a sober desire to chase two legged giants that enjoyed leashing his kind. Slowly, with a sea of persistence the light brown-eyed beast that Joan would later rename, "The walking penis," due to his overly impressive ball-less shaft, found his escape. Unleashed, wearing a tag-less collar, Duke simply hopped out of the car window, stretched, made sure the area was clear, and with a confident jaunt, simply walked away.

At the same time, a movie was being filmed for a typical Hollywood animal production, titled something like, "My Dog the Lab," or, "Lucky and I." The film was a second in a series of movies that would star a Blackfoot yellow lab from Georgia that wore a red collar and was also fixed. If dog's had doppelgangers, this celebrity

8

would be Duke's. The only difference was that this dog's name was Davy and in all honesty sounded about the same as Duke, especially because Davy's trainer on set had a thick Australian accent with a lisp.

So there you have it, two dogs about to trade roles and one dog, sadly getting the underhand. On set Davy had been caged all day and as the humans played out their part in the motion picture the moment came and he was freed, unleashed and walked over to his scene. Davy was supposed to chase his owner through the park and eventually chase a ball and fictitiously get lost in the woods. The odd concept of supposedly fictitious is that once an idea is set free into the universe there is not much stopping a freed fictitious idea from becoming truth. More so in effect, if that fiction is capable of transforming by the soul actions of a common person or fearless dog.

The director calmly says, "Action," while the human runs and then tosses the blue ball far into the actual woods. Davy runs after the ball as directed. After a short few seconds, sees the ball and stops just short of the rubber toy. With the sound of chaos roaring from the film crew behind him and the idea of freedom in front, Davy takes the last few steps to the ball with hopes of a reminder to hold where he came from. Davy picks up the ball and continues to run forward. Only a few pants go by before he smells the bark of Duke behind him.

Slowly turning as to not offend, Duke attacks and bites Davy's back leg. Davy drops the ball in a ditch while running from the beast in a panic. Duke pumps his chest while snatching up the blue ball and heads the direction Davy came from.

Duke clears the woods in no time and in moments arrives on set wearing a red collar, carrying a blue ball. The animal handler screams a name that sounds something like Duke. With promise of a treat Duke walks over, takes the treat and was promptly leashed. Davy on the other hand found himself facing traffic for the first time in his life. Until now he had always been crate trained. The first lane of automobiles was cleared. The second lane a car swerved, until a third driver checking out the ocean view ended Davy's career.

The artists did look for Duke for some time. Unfortunately, the paperwork given to them was for a dog named Jack. Causing the chip number to be wrong. Some posters along with social media proved to go nowhere. The artists gave up unknowingly that Duke was on a plane, drugged, flying to set 101 in California.

Joan and The Man would find out about Duke's whereabouts years later through tabloids on a grocery shelf at checkout. The option to re-adopt was there but so much had changed for the pair of humans, as the reader will found out that Duke was better off at an undisclosed farm somewhere in North Carolina.

As for the two artists, life continued in a quieter place that had less walks around the neighborhood than days before. In all ways, the two had stopped moving in miles together. Now there were more small steps that led to a calm car, with an emphasis on stale rides that ended at trade shows.

Joan was overall happy about her cat no longer living in fear of Duke. The Man, who ceased to be distracted, started to write again, with the replacement of dog treats for favorite pens. All in, the three weeks was fun, with a taste of family life that dissolved in one question that The Man would try to answer over and over, "Was Duke the end of their excitement?"

Chapter One: Joan, Part Two

Meeting The Man

Joan stood four feet eleven inches with flat shoes and five foot even with her favorite brown boots. The boots were a surviving childhood gift that proved relevant as an adult for the reason that her feet stopped growing at age ten. She would wear them no matter the part of year or imbalance of the weather. Her hair was brown with blonde natural highlights that would determine to be difficult when it came to picking a color.

When Joan was young there would be chapters of her hair that morphed into different hues in effort to show a particular mood. Much like a mood ring, the color changed sharply along with the style. Pale but not fair skinned, young Joan wore the sun well; turning olive even after the tattoos appeared. Shy about the fleshy marks their details will remain mute, only that they existed. She was not happy that they would be there for her future kid to see. The man thought of them as a dark memory and was lovingly able to read them clearly. No metaphor or physiological gamble that came from the shadowed bones needed to be decoded.

Joan simply was an angry youngster that reacted visually to the environment, a flat Midwestern locale that in rough truth made her an artist and not dermatologist.

So, that certainty mirroring an idea that was true fades away because of other factors.

Joan was a powerful artist that held thick age to her work. Every line was a multitude of many if not an unusually impossible amount. Her career started heavy and stuck that way for countless towns, states and lovers. The magnitude of the work shrunk with a continual downsizing due to time, life and an energy efficient car. States fell with friends and fellows while the art thinned with the weather, now on her way to life in Florida, paint which was applied to the canvas also seemed less thick. Joan was after all, headed to the sunshine state, where even the artwork wasn't covered aggressively.

Joan arrived and for a time fluttered around the seaside, living with whom she could or had to as long as they accepted her cat as well. Joan finally ended up where she feared and the feline of her young love had attracted vicious fleas.

Around this time is when she walked into the Word Revolt Art Gallery and never left. That possibly is due to her depth perception and a general miscommunication of the 3D world. If there wasn't an item that was fabricated before or during the fifties it was due to be knocked over, dropped or never seen by Joan. She walked in her head and out of luck her body followed. What items or objects happened to be within the three feet of human radius became collateral damage to contemporary thought.

For as Joan walked in to the gallery, she took two steps forward and said, "Hi," then took three steps back, placing her backside to the door. The Man, a little with drink, took off his headphones, smiled, "Welcome to Word Revolt. Are you here to paint?"

Chapter Two: The Man, Part One

Meeting Joan and the Years Before

From the moment Joan walked in, The Man had at best owned the gallery for a few months. The sign had gone up on the street side but the storefront only held a laminate poster stuck to the window with one of those plastic suction cups. Three cement walls with some precariously hung paintings that draped randomly like badly placed earrings on a street person or creative. Not bad, just not pretty or in place to the definition of gallery or competent director.

Thirty-six florescent lights hung with the high beams of massive interruption. Paint, sound and detritus fell around unhip but connected to a hip. Easels stood dragged in weight by tar paintings with others still mixing mediums while they dried. Word Revolt felt fresh in a wet spray paint smell. Items unharmed were left to gather in random lazy spots that were meant for chairs or trinkets of welcoming cheer.

Still, Joan, now through the doorway stayed. Before this night she had looked in, gave notice to The Man's art. The work looked like pieces of someone that she knew. Familiar lines in the abstracts of an intimate face, the colors that a person would wear, Joan knew him rendering the invite weirdly not necessary. So as The Man stood there, as a lost soul in her journey, there was only one question for Joan, "Where have you been hiding?" If The Man was hiding it was from the population first, Joan second and trying to keep his demons to himself third. The latter being an aggressive agitator on multiple scales of the tick releasing charges that is to be alive.

Arguably we live in a more peaceful time but for what violence there is we allow more media coverage. Begging the question if ignorance is bliss, is this time more peaceful way to cause greater casualty without the cost of an official war? What country can afford to lose its working class during a battle over material objectivity? Who would work long hours in promise for the future of more long hours? What people in honest merit fall to the idea that life complete with debt is a well to do life?

Slaves are no longer an option with the same definition attached and that's okay. There is a new trend of hipsters working out the past for those who will just have enough. Tiny living started this way, otherwise known as trailers, living free on grandparents and parents land, all in effort to prepare future generations to be unprepared, to not own land and live in a rent to mobile space. With many trends like this one, there are the lonely that had an untimely time in that chronology of unpopular space where The Man had been hiding before Joan.

That's where the reader will find The Man, stuck in the early years living out time in a condensed space

16

that had zero function not to mention followers or popularity. At this moment, decades passed, without care and vintage was lost to the eighties. This tiny home, built in 1959 had the right solitude, landmark and uncool decrepitness that would later be described by The Man as ready for war, a collection of journal entries completed in the trailer named *The Queen Anne's Harbor*.

Ready for War: Where The Man Was Hiding

Journal Entry One
09/23/2018

In this moment that I am truly alone there is a constant hum in these two ears. A buzz that grows louder when the left and right hand cover their entrance. This sound vibrates low and in the middle of the brain where there should be clarity of thought. That common ground otherwise kept free for the daily inspirations and contemplation. Just as the tree in the middle of a pond provides rest to the winged fowl that would otherwise have to float in compromised water.

The Queen Anne's Harbor trailer has been soberly and drunkenly checked for the pitch but only brown bugs and dog hair were found lurking. Clearly, the sound projected inward and out possibly from the years of electrical devices and the never-ending supply of blue light that the technology of the future provides to the people.

In theory, the only time there was peace from the brain squeak was when there were no electrical devices provided to the body for days. In testimony, that's why the microwave, alarm clock, fridge and AC eventually were removed with the exception of the gas stove. Over seasons of exclusion the hum stopped being noticed unless a vehicle with bright lights took a wrong turn.

Journal Entry Two
09/25/2018

      Moving to a rusted shoebox on the edge of a farm was never the intention or magnitude that was planned to lead to my destiny. A detour to cold showers and a hot night smelling the roses. There is a hang-up in any city's population that blocks a sense of sensibility. Feeding the ducks break and being fed bread is what kept the actions of any free individual well within the fence. Not a high barrier or intimidating one but there mostly for aesthetics and to keep those who are light from falling over to the other side.

      Once contained, the forced acceptance of interaction starts to apply as a controlled mass as we are catered ideas like small business, farmers markets, art markets and the fame of promoting of locals in the community. In effort for those who are enslaved and who have extra income to spend that surplus in aspiration to provide an alternative, mostly at a loss to the other natives in effort to combat the already established corporations. Providing a dream is the best way to keep a working class happyish and productive. The idea is to take just enough that there could be a future in what they are told to do. All in effort to build the perfect continuum until death or being broke takes effect.

Journal Entry Three
09/27/2018

Interjection of others into an otherwise peaceful situation is the undiscovered characteristic that social media has projected on a person otherwise happy to not say hello. Meaning, that it doesn't matter if you are willing to engage with others but others have the sense of right to visit you and yours.

For example owning a dog, if you find yourself sitting on a bench with a dog, all other dog owners will assume the liberty to loosen the leash on their animal and let them visit. Even if the humans and the dog on the bench have no interest of saying hello. If kids or lonely adults find the dog cute, they also approach without reason or care to solitude, this is of course one example of interjection from strangers.

If not dogs, then a simple look, a smile, body gesture or symbol of common interest tops the popularity chart of license to interact with your time and space. An unlocked door or a light on, are other common welcome mats that are typically misinterpreted. Concluding even if the door mat on the porch says *welcome* that in all honesty it is not really wanting you to come in, leaving abeyance of the surrounding world a misfortunate debacle of personal space.

Journal Entry Four
10/12/2018

     Pen and paper can't die from a dead battery but a man can surely perish. Again, the day would seem to have pleasure in repeating the long deeds that were unbearable yesterday. Punishment felt current while the currency had pops and grinds in the fashion of arthritis. That is to say, The Man that might have hollowed wooden shelving now turns to a wheel of unfaithful oak, doing what was done last in a forever attempt to move forward. Fed as a donkey by a carrot this poor vessel lived for signs, representations of foreshadowing that promised the daily spin was not fixed to an axel that belonged to a car on its roof.

     Well placed prophesies on the eve of a dragonfly would only push for a time when the wind blew too strongly for a simple bug to reveal the truth. This story or day as it's called repeats because the actions of this hand will echo. Work, drink and sleep were the identity chosen, by and through again. Meaning without the wordy confusion of poetic overspray, tomorrow will happen as it does on every similar hour and there will be willing participants.

Chapter Two: The Man, Part Two

The Man sits for the better part of the air
conditioner cycle while reading the last journal entry of
Ready For War. That moment in solace with all of the
trailer's windows closed was stale. Even the topic of the
journal entry had exclusion woven throughout. After all,
interjection by others was the grounds of friendship, love
or even a wanted feud. Sitting alone in a tiny kitchen in
pure stillness was the aftermath of rejecting others and
the need for them to take part in personal space.

Often, The Man found a correlation between
what was written and what had to come to fruition to be
impeccable. Attitude had a lot to do with it but living in
Queen Anne's Harbor probably was a major benefactor.
This tin space that had outlived it's warranty was now
turning the pages on yet another. Uncouth, the space
remained safely cheap until there would be a purpose
born to fit the trailer's aged components. Pressed wood
countertops, worn out carpet with the occasional leaking
window, all added to new thoughts finding The Man.

Perspective was really the monster that lived in
the Queen Anne. Untold, that's why he moved to this
exact location, recurring environments led to a recycled
way of thinking that would ultimately drive any lone
individual that was not on pills insane. There had to be a
place that could remove the name of the days and
replace telling time by how tired one felt or the shadows

22

on the wall. This moment of no interjection was eventually turned sour as the air conditioner turned off to give way to the sounds of the evening. Crickets, toads joined in singing with the hum of the rubbing tree branches above. A few times a small branch would break and then land on the metal roof. Sounding like a fairy, tap dancing slightly, then fluttering away.

The Man took a deep breath in effort to remove the worded shadow from around the table and replace the weight with ideas about dinner. Choices included whiskey, beer, roast beef, cheese sandwich or beef jerky. To start, a beer was opened, only to end in the passing of future beers over a canvas that quickly fell ill to an onslaught of mixed points.

Three AM came fast as the artwork laid coldly unfinished, The Man cut the inspiration loose as the last beer vanished. Now, lying in the back corridors of the Queen, the original bed felt stiff in a charming way. The front door was not locked. It never would be for the duration of the stay. Trash had found its way everywhere but the can. All of the front lights were on as well with the exception of the bulb that would burn out overnight. In turn none of the light bulbs would be replaced but simply left to burn out one at a time.

The Man figured when the Queen Anne had gone completely dark that in that moment it would be time to move. The last bulb would travel around the camper, as light was required in different locations. Eventually being dropped in effort to plug in a TV.

Once the television was plugged in there wasn't a need for light bulbs. The blue light projecting commercials flickered just perfectly to cast out the shadows of the trailer. The ad for toothpaste would provide the most light with the least amount of sound. If there was sound it wasn't from people smiling or the paste leaving the tube. No, the vibrations were sexual and if the images had not been there a blind person might assume that porn was playing free, for the racket consisted of men and women repeatedly saying, "Ahh," to the melody of wordless but catchy music.

Other less bright advertisements were for restaurants and libations. Oddly, commercials for mattresses and medications impolitely provided more luminaire. The man had all but stopped writing and lived to the order of commercials that would play around the same time daily. Pacing with a little Earth time during the day when the TV could afford the hours off due to the sun. Dinner was around nine PM, followed by the scenario for sleep, brushing teeth and taking medications was later. Bed was eleven PM when the whiskey took effect.

With the drinking a little heavy, the television became The Man's voice of reason along with the only connection to the outside world that was inescapable. A lot of times when solitude is endeavored the pathological liars lay great detail on the healthiness of being alone with birth. In all honesty there is a prolonged side effect of only having oneself around. Loneliness invades the quiet spaces where thought pauses. The nervousness in general from the conversation that is forced disappears leaving the body to go cold turkey from the natural chemicals the distraction of others bring.

So, there the body sits, acting in recollection to the only way to get high off the drama on television. There are only so many pills to be swallowed with a side of drink before the body goes ill. TV on the other hand is continual with the only hinge being electricity.

Electrical relationships are born and die within fictional characters until all of their Earthly addictions are silenced. Hobbies are not outside of the slain and in fact might be in the center of the very reason that having a trade is not a hipster trend. Along with air cooled cars, organic food that can't grow beards and breweries that allow dogs to sit at the bar. The Man who now sits and waits for a bright denture commercial to salty navigate the Queen to the bathroom and brush teeth as long as the gray hair who is happy says, "Ahh," just before the show comes on and disappears.

Otherwise The Man has to stand in the water closet until the best mattress in the world comes on seven minutes later. Not to say that this moment staring at a dark bowl is wasted. In truth the moment was the only time that The Man wrote short stories. Not on paper but simply in the mind until pushed out by the hurry of returning to the blue light.

There also was a hum that the static window gave. Actually all items that were plugged in had a voice. Coffee pot, microwave, all had a somber tone that welded white noises through the fabric of perfect calm, possibly a plot to drown creativity but clearly that's extreme. To most, white noise is a welcome gift that helps them to sleep. Just as the fan blowing fresh air helps a restless mind, a home plagued with power neutralizes the energy of creative restlessness.

That's where this story has landed. The Man sitting in front of a box of light that freely dictates human schedules to the point nothing is being written down. The very story tucked in a collection of seven notebooks silenced under dust. The Queen Anne's Harbor was now harboring The Man.

In all honestly the aged trailer was the safest place an artist looking to leave the population could do so. If everything in the Queen Anne were not already broken, it would be in a matter of a few liberated nights. As long as the TV played while pushing out the exact thoughts that would rather live on the tip of the tongue than sedated by noise. Months passed with a few seasons and The Man still sat there by the glowing of the blue sun. That bond between flesh, remote and information grew to an unplanned addiction.

Writing was easy but drunk, sitting hundreds of miles from the nearest coffee was easier. Plopped down in some sort of anti creative hibernation became palatable to the taste of passing measure. There wasn't a true sense of identity that came with programs or repetitious jobs. Simple substance did not ask for thought or free will to develop a craft. Staying in the Queen Anne was a ploy to ditch humanity and in doing so, The Man joined the very act of being human in 2018.

Living in society was not the answer but being animated without society while surrounded by all of the vices was worse. Balance was questionable for what happened next but so are the majority of tasks that are completed at night by the light of a twenty inch screen. The mobile home was a small condition of about seven hundred and eighty square feet. In later writings the tiny, pale green trailer would officially be referred to as the Queen Anne's Harbor. Even if the nearest body of water was a Florida retention pond and the only Queen ruled a colony of fire ants living in the shed some yards away.

The Man didn't care that the red bugs lived there because in his mind they kept out larger living pests like Raccoons and Gnomes. They also guarded the never used and permanently rusted clump of Japanese steel that was once a lawnmower. Grass really didn't grow around the Queen Anne's Harbor, due to the never wavering shade of the giant oaks that hung around like old women wearing a lace of Spanish moss. These trees would moan in the wind while they kept the sand beneath forever dry or always wet, depending on what time of year it was.

Yes, for a good thirty or forty feet around The Queen, there wasn't much life at all. Some individual weeds would make a seasonal run at life but their seeds would never take. Most likely it was the noisy ladies and their million miles of established roots that conquered this land. For as soon as the shade of these giants ended a prairie started. Pushed back as the trees grew but large enough to have space to lose and still be vast.

Hundreds of acres of grassland surrounded the small half acre lot that The Queen sat on, once a cattle farm and now a great sampling of the laziness of the modern man, living in the United States. Or an example of how farming here can't compete with the popular brands but most likely a sign of greed that a new generation sold out to a home developer. It didn't really matter for The Man or for this part of the story, because the landscape goes unchanged until he is gone.

Queen Anne's Harbor is a 1959 trailer home that was placed when the home was modern. Not the land of course, but the trailer. The outside used to be sea mist green with Earl White details. The front slanted forward a little and the back was completely flat, almost resembling a loaf of bread that heavier groceries had been stacked on top. At the very front was a window shadowed a little by an overhanging roof. New, the window was tinted but now peeled clearish with only dust to stop the light.

The majority of the Queen Anne's Harbor was wood, tin and glass with some steel for a frame and wheels of rubber for the tires. Four out of four tires had rotted long ago and now were replaced in strength by cement blocks. All hidden by matching green wheel skirt covers. At the point The Man moved in the entire box felt flush to the ground with the bottom of Queen Anne being dirtier due to the wind and splashing of the sand from the hard rain. Three steps made of reclaimed wood led the dweller to a round door with a round window. Resembling a submarine or bomb shelter but weary as a thatched hut.

What held this box strong was not the design but love that was shared here when the grass did grow and the cows grazed. You see, to The Man this was a dirty hideaway that promised to be a quiet place to rot away in introspection. For the Older Man who handed him the keys in trade for nine thousand dollars, this was the dream that started the dream. Yeah, in 1959 this little half acre paradise was all two young people needed to find peace and learn from each other what the world seemed to hide away.

The Story of the original owners occurs decades before The Man came along. There were two youngsters running around the streets of Chicago. Times were what they were. If the reader is interested in the city's history they should go look it up somewhere, for this particular excerpt is only about two. Terri and Arthur, both on the street with the running age of seventeen, had a desire to hear the sounds of night roll into a morning coded in fog.

Now picture this, Arthur is rolling down the street in a car barely running while Terri tries to ride her bicycle in the rain. Arthur pulls over to offer her a ride but when he steps and puts on the brake the car stalls. Terri, a little discombobulated in thought while unfamiliar in her current discouragement from an oil painting she is working on in her mind doesn't notice Arthur's gesture and continues pedaling on through the wet night. Arthur hops from the dead car and runs over to Terri with his coat to cover her from the storm. Terri, of course, upon being attacked from the rear by a shadow trying to toss some dark cloth over her body flinches in surprise.

The sudden flinch turns her handlebars, the tire on her bike hits the curb and all that was already drenched goes splash! She wrecks into a puddle. Arthur stops, Terri is soaked and the rain continues to fall. She looks up at him while her dress flows in the current of the gutter. He looks at her as the once dry coat hangs limp and soaked.

"I have a car," Arthur says. "All creeps seem to!" Replies Terri. "Just trying to keep the rain off you." Arthur replies while looking a little to the left. Terri can't help but admire the try. "It's just rain. Out of everything you can protect me from, this is the most natural."

Terri smiles, "Unless it has nuclear waste in it from the Communists!" Arthur turns his eyes back on the mishap with a smile. "So what's your name stranger?" asked Terri. Arthur takes a moment and replies, "Arthur! What's yours?" She says, "I'm Terri. So you say you have a car Arthur?" "Yes, well, kinda." "It's not big, dark blue and bubbly is it?" Arthur pauses some more, "Um, yes. How did you know?" "Well, Arthur," says Terri, "You had a car." Arthur pauses then replies, "No, I do. It's just not running right now but if you give me a moment I will adjust the …"

`A train horn cries loudly once, twice, and then partially while it cleared Arthur's car clean from the train tracks tossing fiery bits to either side of the road while it roared through the night. "Like I was saying Arthur, you had a car." Arthur paused, "No," He said, "My dad had a car." As Arthur recovered he helped Terri out of the gutter just in time for the water to turn black from the oil in Arthur's Dad's car.

Arthur and Terri stood there in silence while they watched a thousand pieces of the car burn in the field in front of them. The rain had stopped and the smoke filled the space. Terri commented on how the smoke and tiny fires reminded her of driving through Texas and seeing the vast oil fields. Or maybe that was a dream, either way, she couldn't recall.

"Well Arthur," said Terri, "You had better be walking me home." The roar of the city has gone quiet and that means it's getting late. The two walked the first mile of the three mile trip shoulder to shoulder in deep conversation. The second mile holding hands and by the third under a large tree near Terri's house kissing. The fog rolled in and the dew hung around the lovers while the morning light illuminated the water droplets until they shined like hope.

Damp, Arthur walked Terri to her bedroom window and paused. "Stop pausing Arthur, or you might lose something else of your father's." "I already have." He replied. "My first bedroom, breakfast at no cost, a desire to hear his voice. I didn't just lose my father's car last night, the entire man was lost." Terri blushed, "I have a car," she said, "new, a gift from an aunt that recently passed away." Terri paused, "How do you feel about adventures Arthur?" "Ready!" Arthur answered without any hesitation.

After they sold Terri's aunt's car for way more than what it was worth, Arthur bought a pickup truck and the Queen Anne's Harbor with cash. Given, there are some cute stories in between all of that, but this story is not really about them. Arthur swung by with the new living condition. As Terri came to the door she gave a kiss to her mom. Her mom asked where her car was while she looked at the lengthy deathtrap on wheels in front of them. "Mom," Terri said, "I sold her for him."

Mom cried and Terri grabbed her one suitcase, walked down four steps off the porch, ran the fifteen steps to the convoy and got into the truck. Neither would see their parents alive after this point in time. That's okay, Terri and Arthur had sold them for the future of their own lives. It was that or the basement and these two lovers chose a farm field in Florida. Not so much that they chose the field as the truck broke down on a random trip on a road called Queen Anne.

They pulled over and with no direction and stayed a night. One turned into a month, then years. The farmer eventually found them and for trade of the truck sold them the land. While the farmer signed the deed he said, "Glad ya'll found a safe harbor!"

A few days following, Terri painted above the door, *Queen Anne's Harbor*. Before the two moved out they added words with wood that said, *Come Again*. Terri and Arthur thought this would be an Air Bub but when The Man arrived he paid cash for a year and so the sign ended up not making practical sense. Arthur and Terri spent decades in the Queen, finding ways to lessen their time in town.

While they had originally met in the city, the chaos that a mass population produced proved dangerous to their connection. The more distraction, the less time for conversation and deep creation. At the time they moved out the only stuff they had were his writings and her paintings, agreeing that they would only move if they could open an art residency that was completely free for artists. A space that would inspire others to keep pushing their craft, even in the face of constant failure. Not only defeat but the ever present push from outside sources to be preoccupied from ever doing their craft.

If Saturday is for art than you had better believe that the day nine to five wants you to work. Don't worry, you will be paid twenty dollars extra, to work on Saturdays and not follow your compulsion. There are other distractions, kids, spouse, TV, internet, phones, music, getting high, laziness, preparing for work and sleep, to name the ones that seem popular. Side paths that will do everything they can to pull you away, from the blank canvas that belongs to you.

Terri would always wear a T-shirt when Arthur had writers block, on it said, "I don't belong to my parents and you don't belong to your company." Company being the fun word that was played in the quote. In return to Terri's shirt Arthur would wear a T-shirt that read, "Static supply."

Terri was an oil painter and Arthur was a writer as you can tell by now. She enjoyed painting oils of people working in fast food and he would write about anything but fast food, unless you are talking around hamburgers. Arthur spoke in length of their voyage across the country to find the best patty, always agreeing on a few spots in each town.

34

Arthur was deep but Terri was wise. The two were like a covered bridge that would protect each other in private conversation when standing in the public eye. Both would hold guard on either side of the tunnel and wait in anticipation of what the other would send across. Mirrors, with each moment Arthur and Terri took one step closer. Eventually, they met in the middle of the metaphorical wooden cave, where there was only light at either end.

Arthur in the 70s sold his book to a major publishing company that would pay for their dream inside a dream, one that they did not want to leave. Queen Anne's Harbor had been in fact just that. A harbor, a safe place for two young people to focus on what they wanted to do and not what the others asked of them. When Arthur and Terri left the Queen Anne's Harbor, Arthur asked Terri, "How do you feel about global adventure?" Without hesitation she replied with a smile, "Ready."

Here is where we find Arthur handing over the keys to The Man. While Arthur signs the lease he says, "Glad you're able to find harbor here." The Man pauses, "Needed a break from the vacuum." The paperwork is finished and Arthur gets into a green Astrovan, rolling down the window, Arthur says loudly, "Hey! Don't pause too long." Then, drives off with Terri. Arthur and Terri hold the scene until the road turns and The Man is left at the Queen Anne's Harbor. No car, food, or drink, only a 1959 trailer and a fundamental renter.

Terri leans over to Arthur and asks, do you think he'll find it? Arthur, "Depends on your definition of *it*." Terri pauses to hold tension towards Arthur, "you know what I mean." Arthur pauses to hold tension on Terri, the van hits a bump and the old dog Henry groans. Both breathe and toss a happy expression. Arthur pauses, Terri coughs and looks at him unimpressed. Arthur could care less. They've shared too much time for gender guilt, regardless of who started off. Arthur turns at the stop sign and carries the two forward into 2020. Doesn't matter if they turn left or right at that stop sign. Just that they open their art residency. A dream at the end of a dream that is empowered by the color green.

For a spell, there was a slight fear that The Man was a monster, overstepping the situation of what should be a vintage trailer in an effort to crush potential futures. Would this be another casket, with a few lamps, unjust, barely noticed from the far off highway? Over warranty The Man would pass on and the bulbs in the lamps would elapse one by one until the lights all faded.

The energy company would have gone unpaid for some static. Power out of The Man's anatomy would heat up in the Florida humidity, like a bag of popcorn that would cook in the Queen Anne as the harbor would have claimed its first victim. If not for drowning in sweat, perhaps from being forgotten. All at the end of a dirt road in a small town the Chinese call America, buried in a place that has been desperate for life for years. Those not desperate for loners, old trailers, or looking for nothing to do, remained with the town to shop and ignore the decay. They are small in reference but there is much to be said about people who live this way, those who wouldn't want much of anything said about them to begin with.

Seclusion is a journey that's better felt on a personal level. Just as the reader holds the words of this story in their own fashion in minds eye, the voice accent and gender is completely left to creative license. So what does this have to do with you? Probably more than we'd like to admit. You, the seeker for something other than the voice in your head.

The Man didn't necessarily pull out from the conversations of the world as much as disconnecting out of pain or discomfort. Reason is always suggested in this sort of reclusion but hardly ever explained. Darkness, in a lot of ways has as much weight as light, particularly when participating in a slideshow. The Man was not looking to act out of personal gain or feeling of pity from family and friends. No, he needed an adult time out. Time that gave space from bombardment by the drone world in which we are forced to participate.

With every tech toy preparing the populace for a larger tech movement designed to be slightly invasive. Time out retreats will become more and more popular.

This vacation at the Queen Anne's Harbor was the opportunity for The Man to catch up on thoughts and not be advertised to. Groups were a festival, even if there was not a permit or city permission. Sounds, litter, lights, and even the sun became a sign of civilization that threatened to burn. Every occasion was the perfect moment for strangers to get involved in the path The Man would rather track alone.

There is peace when the miles are untethered to others who are always willing to opine company like cheerios in a bowl of liquid. People couldn't help themselves from clumping to get together. The Man in future writings would later term this clumping as the Cheerio Effect. Looking hard onto the easy subject, The Man might have felt a stand if not for the lack of sound that pushed belief to desire in vagabonds. Even tossed turbulence on a more rare occasion between the trees caused a massive space or vacuum that surround the Queen Anne harbor.

Not for the size, of the quaint lot but for the location and placement in reference to the wind and sun. For the trailer sat just right to keep the debris clear from the front door but dark enough to provide complete shade for a long tired man ready for bed around three. When it rained the dark water flowed out from the tree bark above only to land on the front left and pour perfectly from the tip of the roof on the far right.

This bark filled waterfall would flood the various oaks that grew around the giants as a hopefully secluded generation of shades. This did mean that the entire mobile home was at a slant, but the degree to the slant was minimal and forever changing with the growing of the roots underneath. In later points The Man thought, the entire shed rocked when he walked from the back bed to the front bulge that provided the most shade on particular days.

The bench on this side of the rectangle sat under the curved window of an elm green leather bench, built right into the wall. Originally Arthur would sit there and admire the plants, the two of them planted each season. Now the flowerpot was ruled by a small collection of trees and weeds that would bloom but only with thorns and during the spring. Inside the aged shoebox was a bunch of long standing debris. Ideas there were built for thirty years and not much worth a penny past the fifty year mark. Plywood kitchen cabinets now have too many years of the kitchen rainforest effect, drenching the glued construction of mass production.

The floorboards were decent with a few soft spots leftover by spilling bottles of wine and various liquors. Wall textures conceded of ivory and lime green patterns of large and small flowers. The floral motif remained purposefully basic while the colors went from unattended to faded. Above the ceiling hung a loom of cloth dotted with ivory lights now ugly but once appreciated by the original designer. Windows were never cleaned presently and found themselves unwillingly tinted. Towards the rear of the Queen Anne's Harbor rested a bathroom on the right while the one bedroom assured the entire back in all of its twelve feet.

The bathroom was a simple space due to its miniscule size and the color that held true to not cause the cave effect. Basic dove soap sat on the sink, while dripping on the shower in effort to hold tradition in a long standing order with effort to not upset the enzymes in the closely related system.

Out of the loo and into the bedroom the sense of clarity mixed with simplicities ending at the edge of the door kissed by the kickstand. A shaggy red carpet outlines the border of the room while a king lays flat on a wood box upon the fuzzy floor. Blinds are drawn with a layer of dust that had to take a great amount of work. Shelving was also plywood that hugged the kind and only ceased to give way to two small closets. Both currently empty and in waiting for objects to be stuffed inside with almost no care. Books are used to being tossed while other items simply did not matter.

In truth, the entire place was in this jilted state out of neglect. The man could care less about the tactile and its involvement and more for the hands off living that came with living next to a farm that is not yours. Even the removed space gave freedom from the human condition of telling short stories.

40

Small epics in the way we communicate between our daily haves and have nots. For example, the jobs required from people that have left endless small talk are phasing out, facing the moment of how exciting it would be to talk to the living all the time. As the Queen Anne sits between the large oaks so do the people between what's naturally higher than living on Earth. Vertically challenged, The Man sits up in an effort to realize the time of day. He worked the light into shadows on the wall as they helped give into the anxiety that woke him up and kept him up during the night and morning hours.

With no other sense of time in the rear as there were no exposed windows, he had to go by the front glass and what light the space let through. The Man would wake up a few hours before it was due, and watch the glow cascade over the top. Depending on the weather, time or year or even the amount of traffic, forced a false sense of available time to sleep.

If he could have had hours or minutes it didn't matter, sleep never came, only went while it went wild. Lost between wanting to snuggle and feeling pushed to send emails just only after clocking in. If it wasn't for the moment The Man found the gold foil ticket, suddenly there was space to learn to breathe. Now, he was no longer to grit, to live large or push in expense because the funds were there. Queen Anne was what was needed and not a place that wealth like him rested. The Man was actually very wealthy but refused to live in a shrine.

Art tended to thrive better in a humble hand rather than on the hood of a shiny existence. This immobile home that was once mobile was the perfect nest to discover the words that were lost during a structured weakness. A few of the scattered items The Man brought to the Queen Anne included a collection of antique dictionaries that held words which have long been edited out of the vocabulary of modern times. Room had to be made for the popular dialect, especially as the language of the masses shortened in every media that was mainstream. Movies, music and literature have all fell ill during the great shortening.

Words, no matter seen or spoken, have shattered to a herd of three or only two syllables if not one. At this rate future humans will speak through low grunts and base facial manipulations, pronunciations will be mute while tone will prove status and prestige of a person. Quality of the volume of their universal sounds will matter as well. The Man pulled a sheet over flesh and tucked into a dream for the night.

Chapter Two: The Man, Part Three

Happy Coffee

The Man returned to the daylight the next evening around the same time as always. One PM had made the night short while immensely diluting the desired effect of the drink. Waking up continent made last night's revelations less dire to the point another hour was traded in for a wandering conscious.

The Man enjoyed dreaming and did so every night until the point it was uncommon for the dreams to be lucid. Hours lingered as always with little remorse to what needs undertaking. Coffee was brewed with a touch of Irish cream to top the continual bliss of passed hours.

The Man took a sip of the Columbian blend and thought about those tired souls who picked the beans. Another sip, some more Irish cream and the sadness drifted into pleasure. Happy coffee… yes, when this book was finally finished the gallery will also be Happy Coffee. A place that is an excited environment for alcohol induced coffee. Start your day with a kick in the Joe in an undisclosed cup that is there to make the distractions of the world less important. That is until you sober up. Laughing, The Man had four more cups while planning out the Happy Coffee empire. This orphan aspiration would push a hard right for the life of The Man.

Once the buzz returned, work towards rehabbing the Queen as a creative factory began. First order, burn the TV. The television was promptly unplugged and tossed haphazardly out of the door with only a few cows mooing about the noise. Next was to wet wipe the interior and what could be cleaned of the exterior.

Following the great purge, all of the broken or almost broken items were either fixed or completely disarmed for good. This went on for what felt like hours but in reality nine hundred square feet does not take much time to bandage. Lastly, The Man took out the dust crusted writings that were a bit guilty looking if not flat out abused.

Escorted through the fold and past the kitchen table the scripts were commonly placed by the napkins. Pure silence now reigned over Queen Ann's Harbor as all electrical devices had been ejected. Even the trailer itself was unplugged from the grid. There were only three items now existing in that harbor that could make any noise. Pen, paper and of course The Man, standing with rigid fingertips and practically marked notebooks. There were many breaths available to chase, so long as there was a case for the hunt!

Time in this particular moment did pause out of pure anticipation. Balance was on call for long enough to have the sun change drastic position in the sky. If there was a story to tell that had any right it was now the time for inspection. A futile shadow started to fall upon the right side of the Queen Anne. The Man had all he needed to write.

Anxious to translate the falling of shadows on the dwelling the cautious and retired creative had lain dormant to words for months. What was there to say about the rusted draft that would clearly show from an out of practice writer? Would the words still trust The Man as they had or feel crossed betrayal and messy? Could there be an engrossed mind still wanting to toil in casting repetitious lines that ultimately made up the notion of the echoing air conditioner a contender to the sinking sun on the tin box? Hot, speculated The Man of the resistance, as the breeze would not seem to travel lured in by one screen and out the other.

There is a monumental time to debate this condition of sweat and there are moments to rely on instinct. Now swaggering, the soul held back in effort to tease on what was to come if only pen, paper and The Man could have a relationship. Simple at first but containing great possibility to manifest a lifetime of free will, with no advertisements hailed in blue lights.

The Man sat down in a controlled manner and picked up a pen in the same tone, easing into a common starting place. Poetry flowed to help aid the process of a much larger undertaking. Unlike the four journal entries titled, "Ready For War," novellas were easily transmitted onto paper. There was something about being able to finish a walk with the turning of a key that made sense.

Before long there were a plethora of page ideas tossed all over Anne. The Harbor was littered with mumble scumble that had been clogged in the minds eye for way too many commercials. The particular collection would find the title, "Masters of Revels." Unfortunately, only one hundred and one pages barely survived the chaos of the great adventure.

The Man would go on to write a few novels after the literary flash of wordy sewage from the otherwise usable tales. In fact, all together around four books were sacrificed when the editor was married not only to the writer but also to the cause. Without giving away the future, the titles are the only part of those scribbles that are fair to share.

#1 Word Revolt
#2 The Folklore Behind Shade
#3 Masters of Revels
#4 Joan & The Man

Outside of those named the reader will have to hold loosely to the monikers until the year is right for publication. Such works that were inspired by the Queen Anne's Harbor are not for the population but for the one with the pen.

Chapter Two: The Man, Part Four

Word Revolt Art Gallery

The gallery had always been global but never noticed out of frenzy. The Man knew there was a greater use for the idea later described as having a spine. An idea being, "to be free an idea has to be liquid, to be liquid an idea must be free." That being the very quote Word Revolt Art Gallery was built off of. History has always gone to the victorious writers unless freedom is said. The gallery of WR, started by The Man and later cared for by Joan, would stand as the only 100% free art gallery in its state.

To hang, sell, show, participate and to join had only the cost of time and materials towards the artists. WR never took or will take a five dollar bill stiff enough to stick in the wall from a creative. This space, forged out of repulsion of modern trends would stand as the reason people could still dare to create without feeling the cold truth of business.

The Man was very young when the words Word Revolt left the tip of his finger's end. As the truth has potential and cause so does the start of this wordy tale. Word Revolt all started when a tired soul of a middle school teacher assigned The Man one simple task. The teacher spoke, "Students! We will be studying the founding fathers of our country. Some of the forbearers are different now as history has a way of updating itself and that's perfectly healthy for a robust education. We must now drink in the importance of everyone and exclude the reelections from those antiquated texts. That's why all of you will have to buy a fashionable book titled, *The New History of America Volume #1*."

The teacher was well onto her studies but over attached to the new age. To paint her truths brought up more questions than answers, facing the fact that history is a grape vine. Regardless, The Young Man would not have to worry about modern fantasies and in turn focus on the bedtime stories of the past. The assignment was to write a historical outline on the predetermined warrior in time. Out of pure luck The Young Man was handed the name Abraham Lincoln. After a shift of researching this dead orator it became clear that they were at heart one person. He was a poet! The paper was written and turned in.

Simple days later the teacher handed back out the assignments one by one. Thud, thud, thud, the returned papers hit the student desks with a circled grade. Thud, The Young Man heard a pause on the desk attached to the space closely occupied. Her hand rested in front with the paper jostled under pressure of pulsing veins in an old hand. "Young Man, see me after class," the teacher said. Silence filled the classroom as the rest of the students quickly appreciated the grade delivered. The bell rang and the room emptied leaving only one.

The Young Man stood, walked over to the teacher and sat back down in the green chair beside her wooden desk. The ungraded paper in question sat there as well. The teacher said, "Young Man, this paper of yours is wrong. I have no idea where you drew up the inkling that this was a creative assignment. Rewrite this debacle and make it less poetic or I will fail you."

The Young Man replied, "Lincoln was a great poet! This paper was not about what he did but how poetic his deeds were delivered in speeches." In tone, from the Teacher, "Young Man, not everything in life is poetic and you must learn that now." The Young Man took the paper and left the room. A week later the revised paper was back on the teacher's desk. She flipped past the title page to the back only to notice that this writing was now one long poem, slamming the paper on the desk the teacher read the title page, *Word Revolt*. That day The Young Man failed a class and found his cause.

Chapter Three: Part One

Gallery Living

When The Man left the Queen Anne's Harbor there was a magnitude of proclaimed return. Others have never resisted the addicting pull of solitude that lured itself with no responsibilities. Parting meant to take a job that toiled the body as well as the mind until there was only routine remaining. Repetition was their idea that exhausted isolation in the start. Meaning to go back would be giving in to the very paper bag that had been controlling the situation. Still, words no longer flowed, the lights had all burned a final heat signature and the adds from the TV no longer existed to a deaf mind.

Moments came in the form of sitting in the dark listening to the ancient trees above wail their laments. Nature, pristine in all of the ways that it could not be refused, blocked out the roll of thoughts that did not need pronunciation. Sounds of the busy life even started to play out of dreaming. So did popular music along with phrases that had been a thing before casting away from communication. Sirens even made an appearance, clean skin and coffee made by someone other than your self. The mission of leaving was no longer or ever in effect while staging only as a prolonged time that *The Man* had hid from passions.

Time had moved on, yet still the writing, learning or drawing had come to an estimate of notes to accomplish in the Queen Anne, surreptitiously harboring the months. Stains from leaky shelter also helped in erasing previous pages of work. Rain in its very right had taken a liking to the journals of The Man in effort to blacklist the past because there was a lacking future in locked words. Condensation, heat with partial hail had all claimed the time spent in the last few shakes of the trailer by the farm.

Even the cows that stood still for hours seemed bored of the actions falling out of the front door. Mosquito and wasp buckled under permission to the dragonfly and even that bug plotted alternative flight plans. Wind never abandoned the space but from the history of small quarters and gusts that fought in a tragic battle from time that stuck mobile and home together. Static pressure would also fill the air in effect to lift the carpet in the shoebox but had little effect over the shoe wearing. Transition was clearly upon this spot on Earth with only a simple task left to end the melancholy. The Man sat down in the light of dusk with an envelope, page, pen, and stamp.

A letter to the former tenants of the Queen Anne:

Dear Terry and Arthur,

Thunderstorms while living in the Queen Anne have been anything than without sound. Waves of anticipated anxiety have melted in the fear of washing oddly North. The elder trees above have protested this and in moons have fallen discomposed of rot. Cows that once knew the routine of light are now food while the light bulbs are mostly trash. This tin can, your tin can, has been pickling on this lot in many rusty ways. In other notions, this home, your home, has preserved the way people like us travel. For this fact found in consequence not of speaking but watching the trailer fall apart around long crafted writings bring this goodbye. For if we do love each other the goodbye is not forever. If this is an end then know, for all the flowers that presently grow around the Queen Anne, they were never planned or killed. Seedlings growing out of fallen age are that of the never quieting wind over the shy soil.

Darkness was brought upon by lack of buying light bulbs but the TV had a part. Commercials were the real accomplice. Regardless, Terry and Arthur, hope has this ending harbor in need of you both before oxidation wins after the space turns empty on July first. In no intention of abandonment, the time to evacuate while there is a voice to hold clear is here. The surrounding

farm has been sold, the cows and trees cut down.
Construction vehicles are promising condos with intent
of increasing the population on the road by five thousand
or perhaps more. It's now daily workers in hard hats
walk in thinking the trailer is the office, trash is pushed
all around as though this is the dumping site and dock for
everyone who gathers for a smoke break as it's the closest
property offsite. You should see the transition and then
again maybe not. The old oaks roped up with sap for
days while the birds held the skies with nowhere to land.
Deer were being hit with bulldozers but at least the
rodents dine nightly. Bugs swarmed, of the majestic kind
in effort to discover old growth.

Little pines are replanted only to fall under the
hoard of house painters and drywallers. Framers,
construction managers, inspectors, all carved new roads
of noise that killed the crickets' song. Large fires burned
all night to clear the place that this side road use to be.
Winds, floods, not to mention domestic violence now roll
over where rain and animal reigned. There's no longer a
place for a man with a pen. That space, as like all other
natural phenomena has dried out. So, in the manner of
my artist friends before, a city life will be sought out.
Might just be time to open a gallery.

Sincerely,

The Man

Four days stumbled past as The Man was still packing all of the abused items that called Queen Anne home. For not being a person who enjoyed collecting objects there sure where a lot of them scattered around the various nooks full of debris at the valleys.

Mostly books that had various scribbles from lofty moments stretched by longer solitude. At first collecting of all this stuff was fun, then bearable and then daunting. By the end a trash bag had become the preferred method of transportation until even that drew nothing but apathy. With no haste the decision to leave the rest of what was not packed became the preferred method on how to deal with the physical memories.

Now ready, The Man loaded up a green pickup truck with a camper nestled in its bed. The truck was purchased after the letter and had little detail of significance to the story. The Man stood out front of the Queen Anne while still holding on to what the trailer looked like upon arrival. Once attractive the retired home now resembled a beer can that had been tossed from a sour wheel drunk on the side of the road. Distracted, the mailman came driving up and stopped just behind the green pickup.

"Hello there buddy, how are you this evening?" "Leaving," The Man replied. "Ah well, here is your last bit of mail, and here is your last goodbye from me," as the mailman received the seat of his white letter van with a blue eagle on it and left. Most of the parcels stuck in the fingers of the leaving individual were ads or coupons for the local businesses opening shop in the new outside mall just down the road. Tossing those discounts in the mailbox The Man noticed handwriting amongst the heap. It was a letter from a lawyers office addressed to, "The Man," and the Queen Anne's Harbor. Once sheared of its flesh the letter read simply to the point the words sticking to the faint felt cold.

"Dear The Man and Queen Anne's Harbor, The office at law of Pole, Pole & Cube regret to inform you that the owner, Pete has donated the land and property on it, which have been deeded to the Saint Augustine School for the Blind and Deaf. All occupants on this property after the date stamped on the front of the letter are hereby evicted. For questions, please call the number on the letter head or go to polepolecube.com."

The Man felt a sense of retreat but also couldn't help but wonder what had happened to the kindness that lived here. Were they really bad people? Are there such humans that are *bad*? Later the Man would find out that the two that rented him the home were squatters and they actually never owned the Queen Anne or the land it sat on. This would all come about one night in New Orleans when The Man would help a Blind Man cross the street, ending up knee deep at the local bar.

Rousseau's Bar

To the reader this is still the story of how The
Man out of humble deeds meets the original owner of the
Queen Anne and is as important as any bar story told
mid way through a book.

Off to a great start and now wandering The Man
had little plans for a destination or a time that the green
truck had to get there. A few left turns with a general
meandering right ended up in a dumping out onto the
streets of the blue painted town of New Orleans.

At this moment in the evening strippers started to
wander the bricks with their little Persian pimp. Music
also bounced off square clay as every place with a door
was dirty, tired and alive with a band. A few hours are
allotted for flipping through the names at the local
cemeteries. Those too are sullied, drained and with revels
or at least those who were in bands. Exiting the town's
crowds of Uber drivers fighting original taxis fought over
waving hands that jousted others with whistling. People
tripped over lifted sidewalks that played games with high
heels and other heavily drunk feet. Humans of all shapes,
colors and sex plunged around in what looked like an
inside joke from an outsiders perspective. Everything that
wasn't bolted, planted or dead had a rhythm of reason to
move. All but one.

Just there under a streetlight with toes to the end
of the curb stood a man in dark clothing attempting to

cross the street. On one side of the road there were gift shops that held plastic toys for inebriated adults. The side the stranger was going held a lonely tavern called *Rousseau's Bar*. This figure was thin with a gut but wore his fedora just right. Stuck in his hat was a silver pin in the shape of a feather pen. Shades explained the red and white stick that protruded to the ground before him. A few simple steps led The Man over to a man looking to move ahead.

"Evening," The Man's voice cracked out of lack of use. Crossing Man, "Evening to you Sir," voice cracked out of years of whisky. The Man, "Looking to cross?" A line of cars with screaming heads flash by. Crossing Man, "Eventually, eventually I would like to have a drink at the bar over there." The Man, "Let me help you and together we'll have that libation." Crossing Man, "No thanks," stepping forward to car honks the tip of the white and red cane clangs along the side of a furious taxi.

The Man, "Close, if you do make it there, whiskey on the rocks will be waiting for you on the other side." The Man starts to cross. Crossing Man, clearing his throat, "Well! If you're buying then I shouldn't be rude. Take my arm quick, I know the owner and a perfect place to sit."

The two men cross united to the well on the other side of the petroleum vein. Inside The Crossing Man leads them to the booth in the back and a person who looked worried enough to be the manager greeted them. Three, four drinks appeared in a time of an hour on pace with the urgent traffic outside. Before much past short stories, the men found themselves in on an enjoyable night. Long tension broke while ease settled in by the measure of how personal the yarns found depth. Another round floated then sunk the pipes clearing the way for family talk, loss and dreams.

Buzzed for the first time on that particular night a pause landed on the table between them and both looked longingly out across the bar. This must have been the only establishment without live music but rich in conversation. Clearing his throat The Crossing Man tossed back only to lean forward, "Do you have time for a story stranger?" The Man, confused due to the length they had already been sitting, "Yeah, let's hear what you have on deck."

"Every morning I get up around noon and make half and half breakfast. Half coffee, half whiskey. Then, when the mail girl swings by I'm buzzed enough to tell her I love her and she should be my bride. Truth is, it's her nationality that gets me hot. Anyway she is always sweaty from the kiss of New Orleans so any advances are denied. Well one particular morning I had more half than half and the mail ended up all over the lawn. Most of what a blind man receives is useless so the loss was cut and back inside I go. A few cups later that girl helps me

58

sort the affairs, comes in asking about the scattered mail ornaments. She knows I know and we move on.

You know. Then she brings the mail back up. Her name is Tiffany, those are a stubborn bunch if only in the name, Tiff-any. Yea, always in a tiff. So Tiff-any starts going on about some letter she found amongst the discarded bills and coupons saying, Pete, listen to me would you! My name is Pete by the way. Yours?" "The Man," replies The Man. Leaning back Pete opens his eyes and holds resting suspicious face, takes the remainder of the liquid down and laughs, "The Man, my man! Buy us another round."

Drinks arrive so then Pete continues, "I listen to you Tiff-any what's this about a letter?" Tiff-any, "It's from someone called The Man addressed from your old childhood trailer the Queen Anne's Harbor." Both try not to move but whiskey swagger. Pete continues, "What?! I say to Tiff-any. No one has lived there for twenty seven years. Grandma died there remember? What's the letter say?" Tiff-any reads the letter to Pete. The Crossing Man leans back in the booth with a chuckle, "How many people do you think go around calling themselves, The Man?"

A healthy silence stays idle for longer than most pauses of the night. Like thunder Pete leans in close to The Man, "Why were you living in Grandma's mobile home?" Now drunk, The Man tells his story then waits in silence before ordering another round.

Pete takes out a stick of tobacco only to abuse the rolled perfection with fire. A person from the adjacent table explodes with, "Excuse me! You can't do that where they serve food!" Pete blows a smoke ring without hesitation and replies, "Madame, I own the place."

Both satisfied the bartender moves the woman to a different table. Pete finished the stick, runs his tongue over his teeth and says, "So I evicted you, eh? Kicked clean the freeloader silly enough to pay rent to squatters. Then you cross me through traffic and pay for drinks at one of the bars I own! Starting to judge your judgment. Maybe you should rethink how you think."

The Man sits quietly in a way that builds tension in a favorable manner. Pete breaks the moment, "What a night for stories my friend! That old tin can had no value of any sort. Glad someone enjoyed it before the place drowned in condos. Personally, hated it there. Those moaning trees scared the sleep from young blind me."

The Man remained silent. "Well," Pete said, "nothing to add?" The Man, "Thanks for the drinks Pete." Pete, "What?!" The Man, "Signed to the waitress you were paying. Glad the place is yours." Crossing Man, "What! Waiter! What's your name Man?" Silence. The Man walks out returning to the green truck.

Back at the truck there was a welcome sense of quiet remorse. The Man was never into tricking people and less so the handicapped. Even if this particular blind guy was trying to pull one over on the night. In the end of the thought where the brain shuts down and lets the body sleep, The Man felt peace because the drinks were watered down. Any drink that costs nine dollars and consists of mostly water is not worth losing sleep over.

Rising to the sound of the tow truck New Orleans made it clear it was time to move on. After some instant coffee and conversation with the wrecker driver The Man took time to take a wet wipe bath before checking the oil. Now sitting in the cab of the green truck it was time to make a directional decision. Would it be Florida, Maryland or some long road that ended when the engine died? There was plenty of gas that felt short compared to the over patient time of the year. Florida would be hot but there would be plenty of work not to mention a roof by the beach to write under. After a few drive byes of the local recess monitors, their weighty looks were pressing to turn the key and drive. Without a plan The Man aimed the truck towards the sun.

Hours took a breath in between stops at gas stations. Longer on the road brought thought while the trees transformed on connection to the humidity. Rain showers speckled the journey in effort to battle the sun for attention. As the sun won over the rain it lost to the moon while the evening brought heavy eyes that focused on restless legs. Just a few hours into the sunshine state a green sign read *Jacksonville 90 miles*. Knowing little about the civil war and much about sleep The Man decided Jacksonville would be his destination. Shortly, the miles peeled away until there wasn't the decision of what city but which neighborhood. The Man had always enjoyed salt on all foods so in turn aimed for the nearest beach. Atlantic Beach had a quiet vibe compared to Jax Beach and Seahorse Beach sounded drug struck. It was now around eleven with the green truck humming down a four lane road through a sleepy naval town.

Beyond caring The Man made an impulse left turn into a small shopping center. Engine off, lights off, time off, The Man didn't bother to climb into the trailer but curled up on the bench seat up front. The cab quickly heated causing the windows to go down. A dirty shirt was used as a pillow while the rain fought the moon for attention.

Sleep won out until the dreams gathered the sun, moon and rain back in focus. A rising heat of the morning brought the need to rise around six AM into necessity. Drenched in sweat with a mixture of morning dew, The Man cleared watery eyes to look about the parking lot. To the left there was K&T convenience store and to the right a pizza place. The rest of the strip mall was completely empty in a moment of exhaustion. Straight ahead was a vacant space with a realtor sign. The address was 1249 Mayport Road. At that address, Word Revolt Art Gallery would find four walls, one cat, one dog fourteen koi fish and two artists. Just as soon as the space was cleaned, repaired and then noticed.

Chapter Three: Part Two

Honeymoon Adventure

Back at the gallery Joan and The Man are found as they were in the beginning. Both living a life of art. They had once again adopted a dog. He had big ears attached to a small frame and went by the name "Fox". This particular rescue was a German Pinscher that was red, blonde and black in color. Fox's feet were smaller in the back in comparison to the larger paws in the front. Rescuing a dog was a simple one time payment of trust that a human would continue installments on for at least three decades. Fox spent his time with Joan and The Man at every open event and gallery show.

Not sure of what was but preferring the pack life the honeymoon being planned was going to be a tragic event for everyone. To the reader, we now catch up with our lovers on two blue lawn chairs that were rescued and placed in the front center of the gallery. Eating salad Joan made while drinking pecan wine the two creatures chewed their way through planning their honeymoon while tossing a continuously returned toy to Fox.

Joan, "This chunk of chicken is too big Fox, want some?" Fox eats the chicken quickly only to retreat to see if The Man would provide as well. Only with a small rest of the dog's chin on The Man's leg is Fox treated. "We should go to Europe," Joan replies to the quaint sight of a wide eyed Fox. The Man, "Are you suggesting a heritage flight to Eastern Europe?" Joan, "We do both hale from there on all sides and what better place for romance than history?" The Man, "History of our ancestral family?" Joan, "It's not like they will be there. More of an inspirational pilgrimage to discover the roots behind who we are, why we left and the connection of our art and why a gallery could bring us together in the ways only knowledge could define."

The Man, "We'll have to fly over the Alps but that might feel freeing if we plan the flight right." Joan, "Or we could stay here and have another free show." The Man, "We could use inspiration attached to the face of a stranger. At least at the places we have in common." Joan, "Right! Who knows, we might never return."

Both smile at the idea of being strangers in a town packed finely to the rivets with people who were not common. Folks that didn't know their habits or preference on days that were suitable for drink and salad. Where the gallery was in turn was small compared to most places. The miles do not dictate that as much as the friendliness and fact that Atlantic Beach was one beach on a barrier reef, a block of land with the purpose to dissolve storms or keep the energy of the sea away from the inland.

The Man, "Never to return eh? Just the two of us dwelling in a small town full of cheese, wine and strangers? A simple place where neither of us are

64

distracted by work, family or protocol? The only rule being that you and I must be in love to the point cherishing each other's breath over time is pinnacle to a contract that also claims we must snuggle each other at night? Where the two of us could examine one another under the sun and moon's light without competition of the rain or need to ever stand from the well placed bed?" Joan blushes, smiling until her eyes close and says, "Can you get off work?"

The Man looked at Joan in hopes there would be a sign in the two eyes that could buy something related to a pause. A phone barks between the conversation while a ringtone eats away at the romantic mood. Both know that the only person that calls The Man is work. Friends would rather stop by or simply show up to one of Word Revolt's exhibition shows that hid under a title but in the night were revealed as a house party. The Man stood up to check on the pulling leash that also acted as a small window into the couple's life. The apparatus would open between 7 AM and 6 PM at the will of bosses and colleagues. Now scammed, The Man answers the smart phone to find out what fate someone else has in mind for time. The Man is asked to leave town for a week to work in another city four hours away.

The answer is yes, so The Man returns and tells Joan about the delivered absence. Joan is a little sad about the week's loss in excitement but proud that The Man is willing to travel the roads that free her to spend lonely nights with Fox to paint. To be honest, Dinah is there too but the cat is the silent tritagonist. Their prior conversation had now been breathed out of the room in an unintentional attempt to remove the expired oxygen from the space. Both felt an overwhelming sense of sleepiness that pushed the night into a darker place. The Man pulled the mattress off the fold out, blocked the bed from the front window with paintings and the two fell asleep in the gallery.

The Man worked as a home inspector. Every day was spent blowing air through new homes in attempt to prove how energy efficient each dwelling might be. As the technology changed every few months its hard to say if the validity is fact or truth pushed by politicians that have velvet pockets full of change.

Joan's dad would leave for business when she was growing up so departing was always difficult in the back of The Man's mind. Restless, the work needed done and saying yes confirmed a few more weeks of employment. Steady was important at this time while writing was an impulse that was fed by creationism. With the help from a few long nights mixed into a card table, The Man's third book did launch a few days before the work trip.

Forty five editorial posts onto the social market, Masters of Revels took birth out of the screen in an effort to physically hand a copy of the book to those who read. With the story out, The Man woke up around 6 AM, kissed Joan, Fox and said goodbye to Dinah as the road welcomed the four tires of distance. Desired locations were met and the homes were inspected. Some failed, while others fell flat with the occasional passing out of careless distraction that would lay better in the gallery with Joan. The Man finished the day to discover the hotel. Behind the desk a sleepy person checked the traveler in to a room then disconnected. Hotels are weird so the bath, drink and microwave dinner led to a call of Joan that lulled a simple, "I love you too, goodnight."

Next day The Man woke up as always to the cry of the leash. This time it was Joan, "Hun, Masters of Revels sold three thousand last night." "Three thousand?" The Man. "Copies, your book sold three thousand copies last night," Joan replied. Silence. Joan, "You're free, come home."

Joan hung up to let The Man digest what had just gone down. Some research concluded that the book had done what was announced. After a little breakfast wine The Man packed up the wandering belongings and went to work. Finishing the day, The Man returned to the okay hotel. In bed with two sights on the ceiling there was a moment a lone breath never felt so deep. At 9 PM The Man packed once more, drank the rest of the wine, turned over the sheets just before driving home.

The Man walked into the gallery a day before planned. Arrival took one step back when there was notice of her standing there. Two people stood parallel in smiles while dreams trained marathons between minds.

They knew that everything held currently was traded for the three thousand sold yesterday combined with the four thousand sold that evening. Finally, Joan and The Man after a year of marriage could go on their honeymoon without restraint. They booked a one way trip to Austria that night.

Chapter Three: Part Three

The Flight

It's hard to explain why the two wanted to travel to Austria. Joan loved the mountains while The Man enjoyed clear lakes surrounded by cool temperatures. Both relished in day dreaming about castles, palaces and listening to European music. Not to mention Ferdinand Porsche was from there. In clarity The Man thought the area inspiring while Joan wanted to get out of the Florida heat along with getting away from the red ants. Impulse really drove the duo not to mention the small financial freedom that had bloomed overnight.

A honeymoon was always planned but never practical towards the demands of society. It's as if the rule makers passed a common law that having a pause in dialect would be unpopular. Videos, life speech and even relationships are being surgically mutated with the removal of the pause. Every action moving forward must be in a contained chain that never breaks. If the leash did separate, the rolling human would fall from the attention span of others. So no matter what form or sound we choose there should never be silence, a mixture of the two would rule the viewer who only had a few words anyway. With that Joan and The man decided to take a pause to enjoy the sounds of each other completely dissolved from the consonance and dissonance.

The idea was to fly to Austria and then plan on where they would stay, neither fond of heavy itineraries known better as commitment. There was not enough excitement in a premise to outweigh the burden of trying to remember to be at a particular place at a principal time to achieve a boxed outcome.

The paired lovers had also decided to take only one backpack between them in hopes that all the other goods could be purchased as need be. Fox and Dinah would stay with Joan's cousin while the gallery would simply be closed to collect dusty devils. They had no idea when the moment to return would be only, if it wasn't time to leave that they never would.

Especially as the plan for their unborn daughter Winter was being drawn out in a more serious manner than just talking. In every way Winter would live the life Joan and The Man had dreamed about as youths. She would be what she wanted and nothing more or less. Winter Joan Rykaczewski would change the world or at least have a great antiquities collection at Word Revolt.

September twenty seventh around two PM came rapidly for the young married couple as they rushed off to the airport. With backpack in hand the young Uber rider did their best to keep the traffic mixed with late tension towards a happy occasion. The Driver, crossing lanes after the edge of their seat gels over inbound traffic, asks, "Where are you two wondering?" The Man, "What!?" The Driver, loudly, "Flying?" "Yes!" Joan

70

answers. "Where to?" says the driver. The Man, "Austria." "Really!" the driver exclaims, "Always wanted to go down under." "No, Austria, it's in Eastern Europe," says Joan. Driver, "Oh. Cool. Sounds cold." "Peaceful," from under the breath of The Man. The Driver, "What!?" "Nothing, what's your name?" Joan says. "Never been," replies the driver. Joan asks again, "Your name?" The driver turns down the radio to kill the commercial, "I'm Juniper. You?" Joan, "I'm Joan and this is The Man." Driver, "I feel like I know you two from somewhere."

The music is turned up after an awkward pause while the car plunged through the air. Arriving at the airport Juniper smiles while The Man and Joan unbuckle. Juniper, "Have a safe trip! Really hope you two find what you need out of Austria." Joan, "Thank you, maybe we will see you on our return home." Juniper, "Yeah, when's that?" Juniper, Joan and The Man experience a long pause, "We don't know."

All the doors are closed then, as Juniper directed the car a few more feet and picked up a guy. Joan and The Man could hear Juniper say, "Welcome, what's your name?" The stranger hobbles over, "I'm Thaddeus." Juniper, "Where to?" Thaddeus, "To meet... someone." The car door closes and the two drive out of sight.

The honeymooners smile at their union, holding hands in departure into the airport. Excitement could be felt in how fast the clasped hands warmed as they began to sweat. Quickly retrieving their tickets from a robot the duo made their way through the proper checkpoints in a glossy manner. With plenty of time to absorb, Joan suggests they grab a beer in an attempt for a buzz before the long flight. A decision was made to stay close to the tarmac gate as there was a perfectly fine wine bar and royalties to watch nearby.

Joan, "excited to leave the country for the first time besides Canada?" The Man, "distance from all of this mixed with culture shock actually sounds refreshing." Joan agrees, "The distance will be great! Do you know what you'll write?" The Man, musing, "No. Maybe the beer will be so tempting that all the time will be spent watching you Plein air watercolor moaning volcanoes." Joan, "Yeah, you could use some rest."

The drinks active, both ordered sangria with a cheese plate to split. They enjoyed mostly the same foods and the rare moment they did not the disconcerted palette would eat a particular taste until they merged. Again, Joan and The Man were not sold on forever unless it was their love for one another.

Joan, "At least this flight won't be like your second book." The Man, "Right?" "Although, the adventure was phenomenal," Joan, "your friend The Old Man almost killed you both!" The Man admitted with a smile, "True, but he did get us to Canada in time for the interview on Folklore Behind Shade." Joan laughs, "Ha, just jealous I wasn't there! The Old Man really has bee there for you." The Man, in reminiscence, "He was a great pilot."

The Bartender brings the second round to Joan and The Man while accidentally overhearing The Man. The Bartender, "Did you say The Old Man? Sorry to interrupt but I've heard of him. Some life he flew!" The Bartender was thin with a pointy nose that protruded between two blue eyes. He had worked the liberated scene from the time of a young bar back. Now well traveled, the Bartender enjoyed working at airports due to the stories rambling travelers had leisure to share. After a while there did not seem to be a point if the wonder didn't have a face to bounce their miles off of.

The Bartender had a black shirt that was tacked onto jeans that ended in boots. A mix of joy and sadness that he tried to kill with sheer hints of intrigue that moved like a disturbed fog. Leaning over the counter while grinning the pause eventually ended with The Man saying, "Okay, The Old Man would be one of the destined reasons this particular voyage is happening."

The excerpt unfolded from The Man as told. "You see, there was this great chance to be interviewed by a popular art magazine in Canada. The entire trip on a commercial flight would take around one week. That evening when the interview opportunity found its way into ten boxes there was a hope for what was to come. Finally, there would be an outcome of all the writing that flowed. The only issue being that the full time job that paid for the gallery would have to let their worker go rogue for a few days.

That phone call to the boss was made with a long explanation that used words like dream, opportunity, passion and freedom. The last word might have been a mistake as the Boss replied in a PR way that hit as a simple no. The system said the number that represented time off in the personal bank of The Man was zero. The Boss finished with, maybe next year. That's where The Old Man comes in.

A particular elder gentleman, who owns a plane, had asked me once if the moment was right. He had extended the invitation to join him on an adventure, one that would take us across lakes and through great moments of well needed danger. You see, The Old Man had this thought on how danger was what held people responsible for living. Not love, sex or family but the fear of going through some event that could potentially destroy a person.

That very thought is why The Old Man bought the aircraft that he did. If the plane were too big the risk would be less but if the sky craft were too small the jeopardy would be so great that he probably would have not lived long enough for more perilous situations. To hone and prove his theory even further to the observer, The Old Man even named his ship, *The Danger*. Not the first choice for many pilots but that was most likely brought upon by age.

This wrinkled soul had lived well, in fact, everything that needed accomplishing had been done so early in his life that time itself expanded. Money, kids, a wife and even happiness all fluttered in his early 30s and then made their own way into the world. Including his wife who had a near death experience on the Danger in the earlier years of their marriage that led her to leave to be with a librarian. The Old Man was now alone, but constantly surrounded by people looking to hear a good story and possibly living through the long tales of a massive life well lived. For many of us we do not want fame and fortune but a quiet place in time where we can nest in routine while the comforts of nothing sooth over the majority of the days."

Never someone who was comfortable in flesh and space the need for generic days did not feed The Man at first. His relationship with The Old Man was actually an attempt to drive out the staggered waters of the being in which his energy was confined. Nothing had ever come so close to exemption for The Man than the friendship that thrived off of conversations about danger through the act of flying. The invitation from The Old Man would not have to be perfect or even detailed for an agreement to be reached on such a voyage that might kill or severely scare the participants.

Out of desperation for more the call to barely survive was always on The Man's mind and yet the years continued to ebb and flow while The Old Man grew older with no sign of an invite but only stories. All of the time spent with The Old Man was in story with no opportunity to interject a self sent invitation. Most likely this was on purpose, as everyone he knew long enough to tell the tale wanted to go on one of the many described exploits. Probably because the friends had assumed the ending and that everyone survived. Unlike them, time was limited and the next breath they talked there had to be action of daydreaming about what was, a moment in reality that required a inhale from mother nature that would slide over the wings of an old man's aircraft.

From wavering reverie, The Man continued, "This time, our conversation had to be painted with no stories, only a plan to get to Canada and back in three days!" Completely possible, as Google said that the duration of the flight would only take around five hours and fifteen minutes.

On the way to the bar, *Wings*, that was located in a small airport just about an hour inland on A1A, the thought of a firm asking attached to little threat would be The Man's ticket for a ride on Danger. Arriving, The Man found the legend like he never left. Perched on a sky blue stool was The Old Man surrounded by travelers and air people. This story was told before, so there was a pause of interaction prior to the long anticipated approach. The Old Man finished a drink while the crowded zone bought him around the dissipated scene.

76

Walking over in a rare silence the two were excited to see each other and before an order could be made The Old Man said to The Man, "Ah, have I told you of the moment a drunk cross dresser almost drowned all because They had dressed like a mermaid and..." The Man, "Stop!" The Old Man, stopped looking into space while wrinkling his face.

The Man, "Your stories are epic but it's time we make one of our own. Here to Canada and back in three days. It's possible, just say yes!" Old Man, wondering why in a sudden outburst replied, "Drugs, wanting to fly in some drugs?!" The Man, taken aback, "What? No! This is a chance on destiny!" There, The Old Man was told a story with words like dream, opportunity, passion and freedom.

Once the tale was over, The Old Man turned forward with a bleak face while he completed two rounds with only digestive sounds as he considered the forthright proposition, resounding in, "Son, I haven't flown in over a year. If my blood sugar crashes and I fall asleep... So will we." The Man turned forward with a smooth but bleak face as he finished the warm beer. The Man, "We won't take Joan. Just the two of us in Danger on one last mission! If you fall asleep then everything will be done to get you up while these hands work to fly your ship." The Old Man, amused, "Ha, you don't know how to fly and there's a clear difference between danger and stupidity!" The Man, "Is sitting on a bar stool, the last tale you want people whispering about you? Oh yes Sir, The Old Man was really great. Spent all of his last years sitting right there getting foggy."

The Old Man turned away slightly to end the conversation. Driving home with the rejection was the longest haul The Man has had since the trailer. This started only to end before there was a beginning. On the following day, the interview would have to be turned down, breaking a little chip off of rare hopefulness.

Morning came and the backpack sat there still packed ready for a choice. This was the day, if there was ever one to find a way to hogtie The Old Man. The Man was back on the road to the airport collected and willing to try once more! Walking into *Wings*, The Man stopped, looked around and then noticed he was alone. The Old Man was not on his stool.

"He's out in the airfield," yelled The Bartender. Chills overcame that produced a mass rush to the strips of blacktop that held pinned birds. There stood an old man smoking a cigar playing with his engine. *Danger* was running! Watching The Old Man hobble down the ladder, then walking over to a small table that had a bottle of old cask whiskey resting on it. The bottle was half full until he gave a mighty chug to toss down another round of multiple shots. Out of the reflection of his plane The Old Man saw The Writer standing there.

"Ah! Good morning, want some breakfast?" asked The Old Man, holding up the bottle. The Man, smiling, "Absolutely!" The Old Man, "Delicious, don't worry there's more on board. In fact, it's all I packed!" The Man, in excitement, "Awesome, so we're going?" The Old Man, with ardor, "Yes Sir! And in style! Why don't you load your bag and look around the inside of Danger." Once inside the airship the surroundings looked as if an ostrich had nested in the plane.

Maps, bottles, clothing and trunks full of who knows what was littered throughout the cargo haul. With a thump The Old Man appeared next to The Man. The Old Man, "What did you expect? Danger and I have been bachelors for well over forty years!" The Man, "It's perfect.

The Man, selling the story once again, "Both of us sat buzzed while the destination was mapped. Then a clear voice came over the antiquated radio. "Danger, you're clear for take off. Keep your eyes wide and liver sharp!" Neither ready nor truly not prepared we ran around Danger tossing in the remainder of the random supplies that had been sleeping on the tarmac. Within two minutes the craft was raring forward towards the take off lane. The Old Man, Danger and all of its contents went racing down the runway fueled by ambition and whiskey. Then, flop, The Old Man started to nod before the wheels had ever left the ground. Panicking The Old Man suddenly raised his head and the plane's wheel at the same time! The aircraft launched into the sky in the fashion of a great, frightened fowl! In zeal The Old Man shouted, "Here we come destiny, oh destiny, meet Danger!"

To his wrapped audience, now including various eavesdroppers, The Man kept on, "We were about an hour into our flight, dissolving long glances through faded windows when the wonder cleared. The Old Man, "Why don't you go back to that green trunk and get us something to drink then." Unbuckling and making way to the back of the craft would come to be the easy part. The trunk was dusty until the point of being beaten senseless. Inside, bottles of whiskey where lined up haphazardly in square crates. Lifting one out then closing the chest, the soles of my shoes that were stuck to the plane lifted in a free fall!

Letting go of the bottle it smashed against the wall along with everything else. Danger was spiraling downward with The Old Man asleep at the helm. Possibly passed out but definitely not returning anytime soon. Fighting to crawl to the front, a great force we know as gravity assuaged back. Yelling at The Old Man, an ample blue lake now filled the entire view of the windshield. Get up, please! Papers danced with maps all around the dreaming pilot until an empty bottle bounced off his head.

The Old Man shuffled awake while stretching as if awaking from a peaceful dream on a sofa." The Man, "Pull up Old Man!" The Old Man, rubbing glazed eyes, "A Lake!" With a mighty yank the ancient bird groaned

80

alongside The Old Man, leveling out just in time to scrape the surface of the water only to slow seamlessly to a rest. The Old Man could see the worry cast over The Man's face. The Old Man starts laughing, "Danger is amphibious." Shuffling around the mess he found a bottle to drink before returning to the controls, trolling the plane over to a dock then kills the engine.

The Old Man, "We're making great time. Let's tie down and have lunch."

Eyes meet The Man, "As you could imagine the thought of lunch was definitely not around. Still, we hopped out of the plane onto the deck that led directly to a restaurant." Being seated right away the waiter walks over, "That was one heck of an entry boys!" The Old Man, "Ha, that was to teach this hitchhiker how it felt to be in the war! When I flew out of survival we had to land anyway we could on a moment's notice. Sober too if you can imagine that." The Waiter, astonished, "So, you did that on purpose?" The Old Man, "I still have my appetite don't I? Let's see some menus and a drink list."

"To this day the thought of The Old Man landing the way he did still haunts me. The rest of the trip went smooth until it was time to come home from Canada. Not that it matters but the interview went well too, with more than a few copies being sold because of it. Anyway, once arriving back to the airport in Canada, the bartender at the *Winged Leaf* informed me that The Old

Man had already flown away, "Yea, he's taken Danger to the skies but he did leave you this letter."

Dear The Man,

I hope this letter finds you sober so my gift has a purpose. The skies have called Danger out into the world because of you! Thank you for pulling an old man out of oblivion. There's a charter waiting to fly you home tonight. When you're in need of some Danger you'll know where to find me.

All the best,

Danger & The Old Man

The charter flight back was boring but not sober while the sky felt empty without the sounds of The Old Man and that bucket of rivets. In a swift draw The Man finished a gifted bottle of memories. About three months later we caught up at *Wings* and had a story to share with the pilots and travelers. The Old Man now flies every chance he gets. As we are on our way to honeymoon in Austria, we figured it would be safer to leave Danger out of this trip.

The Bartender, satisfied in his choice of entertainment, "That's one way to chase your dreams!

They always say to never give up on a person telling you no. I've always wanted to be a sommelier but never found the time or money. Oh well, here's your receipt please pay the cashier at the front."

Joan and The Man smiled because the receipt was for $27.47 and both twenty seven along with forty seven were lucky numbers for them. Once settled for the two gathered themselves, pulling clothing while adjusting to standing after sipping on the last of the water. Care was passed along edges in checking for spilled debris before reaching their flight information. When they leisurely arrived at the gate everyone was already gathered to stand with other strangers in excitement.

Neither Joan nor The Man enjoyed crowds, now wishing they had dwelled at the bar with the story. Half an hour passed through people watching for an end that would result in more sitting. Cattle finally were given the prod to merge through the gate onto a tin box that had a pilot escorted by two stewards etching to move fast enough to fly. The artists found two seats together, right away then landed before theft. The shared backpack was tucked between The Man's legs. The two held hands while ignoring the honest terms of chaos that swung around the cabin. Nervous energy settled to only be replaced by quiet nervous resolution.

The Captain of this airborne greyhound said his speech about safety, then moments later the airbus was entertained by a happy stewardess talking about what to do if we fall from grace. Everything was said but how to pray, instead we taxied out. Trust kicked in, tossing all two hundred and twenty seven passengers into the air. Joan and The Man where finally on their way to a long postponed honeymoon. Earth vanished to be replaced by clouds spotted by tubes of humans.

Joan fell asleep on The Man's shoulder while they tossed through lower space. Nine hours and a barrage of extra seconds had passed with the majority of the shipping container asleep. The Man was journaling while sipping on overpriced drinks that came too infrequently. This airlifted room was peaceful to the point calm had risen in familiarity. For once there was nowhere to go or a time that needed to be kept. Joan opened her sleepy eyes and kissed The Man. "I love you," came from young lips as she settled back into the arms of safety. From there, all of the ugliness of the modern world had been left behind.

A beep rang out, BEEP, BEEP, BEEP. Flash of white light filled the cabin and neither Joan or The Man could feel the other's hand.

Chapter Four: Crash Utopia

A soft touch ran over Joan's face and when she opened her eyes it was The Man smiling down.
The Man, "It's all going to be okay Joan. The plane had a malfunction and crashed." Joan, confused, "Oh no! Is everyone alright?" The Man looked around, "Not sure, the wreck is far away. We must have been tossed out before the worst of it."

Joan and The Man where sitting in tall grass that carried over the valley to the base of mountains. By the looks of the surroundings they were in the foothills of Austria. Neither one of them was disabled past a bruise. After some time that helped dilute the shock of falling the two sat in each other's arms to enjoy being together with such an amazing view. After a few long moments of thankful relief wonder grew restless out of guilt. Joan, "Let's get up to see if anyone needs help." The Man, "Yes and look for supplies or a town."

The two stood to start their treck across the valley. Oddly there wasn't a single sign of the plane let alone any other meandering survivors. They were by the looks of things completely alone. Of more luck however was that the weather was perfect with an ideal amount of sunshine and cool wind. They even had this prolonged sense of fullness mixed with content that blossomed out pure happiness.

After a shift Joan and The Man came across the snack cart that had need on the flight. It was the only object that would be found after hours of harmonious exploration. Joan suggested that they have a picnic to rest a little before going on. For some reason there wasn't any sense of urgency or rush to be saved. All they wanted to do was enjoy each other's company in the moments with no one around but their love that drove long conversations mixed with perfect pauses.

They sat upon a large rock that they covered with a tiny white blanket. Miniature bottles of wine paired with portioned snacks complimented well with the overwhelming surrounding mountains. The Man reflected on the day Joan walked into the gallery. Joan laughed while she told the story about the first time they painted the same abstract together. This back and forth carried them to the day's end.

Descending from the rock to the soft grass below they repositioned the blanket on the ground, on their backs staring at the sky as the sun went down to be replaced by the stars. Cuddling the two creatives fell asleep to the sound of the wind carrying a fragrant smell of wild flowers. This particular night wanted to last forever in the artist's hearts. That night did last particularly long if only to prove that this world could still be perfect.

With the dawn Joan and The Man rose out from their dreams. Another perfect day hung by the sun as they collected themselves. Joan, "Where should we go?" The Man, "Not sure but look over there, seems to be a path of some sort. Maybe Deer? Joan gathered snacks on a small plate then handed The Man a beer. Once all of the drinks were finished from the cart the happy couple walked hand in hand down the random trail. The road that was probably an animal highway was surprisingly beautiful with never ending places to stop and admire the glory of nature.

There were waterfalls, large rock walls speckled with gems that caught the light that peeked through the overhanging canopy. The ground was soft with moss but not muddy so walking was pleasant to the point miles passed without any tiredness that would normally bring fatigue. If there ever was a perfect hike then this honeymoon meander was it. The only instance they stopped for a stretch of time was to embrace a cool mountain spring, both lying intimately by the rushing virgin water watching brightly colored fish swim about. Joan and The Man had now walked for hours through memories of their four short years together.

They also dreamed of a future where The Man would write while Joan chased Winter around the yard. All Three would live in a converted library in a secluded town up North in days filled with home cooked meals paired with music and art. Culture would act as the heartbeat of the homestead. Winter would be homeschooled while raised going to public events that were inspiring or simply engaging. Joan and The Man would continue their impulse of painting with a monthly house party to show their latest creations. Fox would grow old with his brothers that would mature from puppies into full size Dobermans.

Time would only be a muse at best as neither would be constricted through the lack of resources. Years acted as milestones to the never ending cups of coffee that were full of cream for her and whiskey for The Man. Yes, this honeymoon was only the beginning of walking down many paths in what was sure to be Utopia.

Once again, light had started to fade as the path began to widen revealing a clearing. Joan, "Look, there's a structure ahead!" The Man, "Hey, that looks promising. Let's check it out slowly." Shoulder to shoulder they made a way forward. The building was large to the point parts grew out of sight the closer they came. Perched on the banks of a glass clear river that spun a large mill wheel. They had come across an old hotel that was primarily built out of stone attached to German wood. The spinning mill must have powered the entire thirty plus room shelter.

Joan, "It's..." "Perfect," finished The Man. A place as this had always been in the back of their minds as the ideal refuge to stay deep in craft. The hotel had signs of abandonment but not disrepair. Joan and The Man walked close until the tips of their shoes touched the front of the steps. Twenty steps lead to a wrap around porch holding multiple doors with one large oak entrance in the middle. Rocking chairs covered in leaves rocked slightly in the cool wind that passed warm air. Step by step with their hands clenched, Joan and The Man walked up to the front door.

The Man, looking to Joan, "Do the honors?" Joan placed her hand on the elegant cast iron door handle made to resemble a rose. The heavy door clicked then swung poetically slow inward without a sound. Deep breaths guided the couple inside. Out of the darkness shadows aided the light from the large windows, providing details about the space. No one was obviously here or had been for the majority of at least a decade.

The Man let go of Joan's hand moving towards a grey box on the far wall. With a push the attacked bulbs flashed on while others exploded. This sort of excitement made for a romance more than fear. The sudden flash resembled watching asteroids enter the atmosphere only to explode in bright colors of fire. The Man, "Ha, that was brilliant!" Joan cheered, "Honey, I loved that!" Now lit up, the space showed true character.

A long bar, hand carved, lined the wall to left while a stage of chairs and an old piano hung out to the right. Heavy stairs made a way to a landing on another landing that led to the rest of the building. At the head of the climb was a stained glass amphibian aircraft that radiated a greyish blue light.

With a smile on The Man's face the bar was completely stocked holding every type of drink one could taste in a lifetime. Joan walked over to the piano to find a stack of coins. She took one of the coins and placed it through the slot in the box attached to the old sound. A few clicks later the ivory keys began to move while music filled the atmosphere. A joyous song that mysteriously resembled American folklore vibrated outwards.

Joan, "Imagine That!" The Man, "Want a drink?" Joan, "Absolutely!" Music dancing around the room, The Man cleaned the dust from two glasses then filled them with a loving mixture, whiskey with a splash of cherry flavor. The two toasted to health, wealth, happiness and Word Revolt! That night was spent floating in a cheer on the moment that was to be their future. Hours passed as the light that traveled through the window moved from the wall to the floor until disappearing altogether.

The Man, "We had better find where we are going to crash." High spirited grabbing, they clutched each other's hand as they made their way up the stairs to the hallway of doors. Each door had a faded pastel color with a unique stained glass light to illuminate the number of the room. With no hesitation both ran down the hall to the Fox light, room twenty seven as fate would have it. The unlocked door gave way to open and close with ease. Leaving the reader to imagine what happened on the other side.

Next morning the two creatives rose out of bed in anticipation to explore their lover's hideaway. Still hungry they drank a little wine while they went on to meander. There was a great library holding vintage books from all over the world decorated by long reading stations. Each table was adorned with stained glass lamps that reflected famous literature. The ceiling was glass, providing light to large pots below once holding even grander foliage. Joan's favorite was the atrium on the roof that must have been a spectacle in its years.

Nothing compared to the drawing room of course. Stuffed with canvases, diaries, paints of every type holding all colors imaginable. This particular room was massive with impeccable luminescence falling onto giant sofas paired with puffy chairs. A Victrola machine sat rested next to a small wet bar with a cooler once holding food. Artists could have spent a lifetime creating in this space and never run out of supplies or even dream of a project too large. In the middle of the room lived a blue wire spindle converted into a table for parlor dice. The Man walked over to the round table to see the sleeping book on the surface. Lovingly left, a letter lay flat with precise folds on top of the book. The Man unfolded aged parchment to read.

To whom who finds the found,

When talking about what happened in this hotel it's hard to leave out the creativity. This refuge was once an art residency that two young creatives dared to imagine in a wide awake dream. The very best painters alongside writers have emerged from these walls. The program was famously called The Word Revolt Project. Young mixed with old and every gender intermingled into every nationality, all coming from around the globe to study alongside two directors. Experimental, classical, abstract to name a few filled this completely free expression of social change.

All a human had to do was apply, once accepted everything was free. Supplies, boarding and food flowed at no cost as long as they were participating. Once a month there would be a massive party to celebrate artistic freedom. Generations would find their path from this free space. They would leave behind the implanted notions of an ugly world in an effort to strike a change in the hearts of people from every walk that this blue ball we live on can offer. If we would simply slow down in a united manor to tell those in power that we will not work faster than our extension, our slavery would shorten if not conclude. In fact we will from now on take the needed time to enjoy the moments of the day. Earth is not a work camp it's our home. Only when the collective believes in this will the race turn into a celebration of life!

92

All is possible if the able take to heart the carving out of small connective beacons that can be merged to form one light forward to stand as Utopia. We did that here. The love of my life and our role in creating a world that a child would find pleasant measure when born. It's now your turn to find the empowerment and be the new voice of Utopia.

Yours,

Charles and The Woman

9.23.1907

Hard to believe all of this had sat for so long untouched. Joan came over to read the letter only to feel greatness with a slight tummy ache. This was the first time either one felt discomfort. Joan sways a little and The Man catches her. Dizzy, The Man carries Joan over to the nearest puffy chair. She sits while The Man kneels in front of her. The Man, holding Joan's hand, "Was hoping we had more time Joan."

Joan, "I'm fine, must be all the drinking that's all." The Man asks, "Do you like it here?" Joan, "Miss eating but yes I love it." The Man, "This is the life that will be for you and Winter." Joan, "Oh? And where will you be?" The Man, pausing, "With you, right here. Holding his hand to her heart." Joan, laughing, "You're already here." The Man, "Promise me you'll build that Utopia that you've always described. Let Winter know that this world is poetic and that there is always a way to find beauty even is she has to be the one to create it." Joan, "Of course. We'll be great parents together." The Man smiles then leans over and kisses Joan's stomach, "I love you two."

Everything goes dark to the point Joan thinks her eyes are closed. With a shake pain hits her entire body as a warm liquid runs all over her face. She opens her eyes and sees a smoke filled sky. Screams echo from every direction. Red helicopters rush around resembling dragonflies. Joan goes to move but as she sits up blood shoots from where her leg once was and she lands horizontally. Shock sets in as her left arm is lifted to remove the hair from her face but only a bone and elbow rise to meet her eyesight. Yelling. "The Man! The Man! Where are you!?"

Her eyes close to meet the sound of A Stranger's voice moments later. A Stranger, "Over here! She is alive, quick!" Before Joan goes unconscious she hears the paramedics talking. From Parametric One, "How did this happen?" The Other Parametric, "No idea, it's like the aircraft just exploded and fell out of the sky, news reports it's a software issue." Paramedic One, "How many survived?" The Other Paramedic answered, "So far, just the two of them."

Three Months Later

Joan arrives out of her coma to an optimistic hospital staff member. A nurse stands with multiple doctors to welcome her back to consciousness. "Joan, can you tell me your name?" says The Doctor. Joan, "Where's The Man?!" The Doctor, more insistent, "Your name first please?" Joan, "Joan, my name is Joan. Where is The Man!?" The Doctor, "You've been through a lot. Rest for now and we'll be back with details."

After some time The Doctor returned and informed Joan she was the only survivor and that was especially a miracle because she was also pregnant with a baby girl. That and all her limbs were able to be reattached. Joan spent the rest of her term in the hospital asking about The Man. Unfortunately, they never found The Man or any sign of the backpack.

Winter was born January 12th at 2:47 PM weighing in at three pounds seven ounces.

Joan would recover with the help of rehabilitation and eventually buy an old hotel from the compensation received from the airline company. Winter grew up with The Man's love of writing and her mother's natural gift for painting. With those skills, Winter would go on to be a best selling author for her work in Utopianism.

With fame she would call to arms a peaceful revolution towards capitalism. So much so that modern culture stopped focusing on the end of times and began idealizing the future.

For Theresa and our future daughter, Winter.
8.5.19

Made in the USA
Columbia, SC
05 June 2020